MASK OF EVIL

by John Hughes
illustrated by Al McWilliams

A GOLDEN BOOK • NEW YORK
Western Publishing Company, Inc., Racine, Wisconsin 53404

There was great excitement at the Royal Palace of Eternia. The Lady Irena had come to visit, and she was an important guest. She had been childhood friends with Prince Adam and Teela.

When Orko, the court jester, happened to pass the lady's chamber, he saw a surprising thing. Irena was sharpening a dagger!

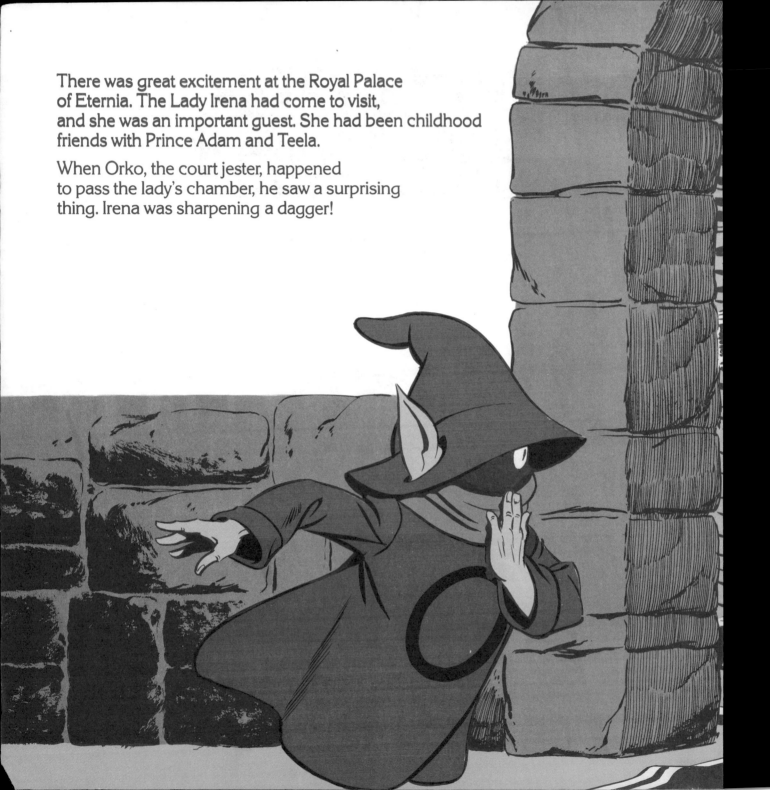

That evening there was a royal banquet in honor of Lady Irena's visit.

Orko said nothing about the knife, but he was still puzzled by it when he was called to entertain the King and his guests at the banquet.

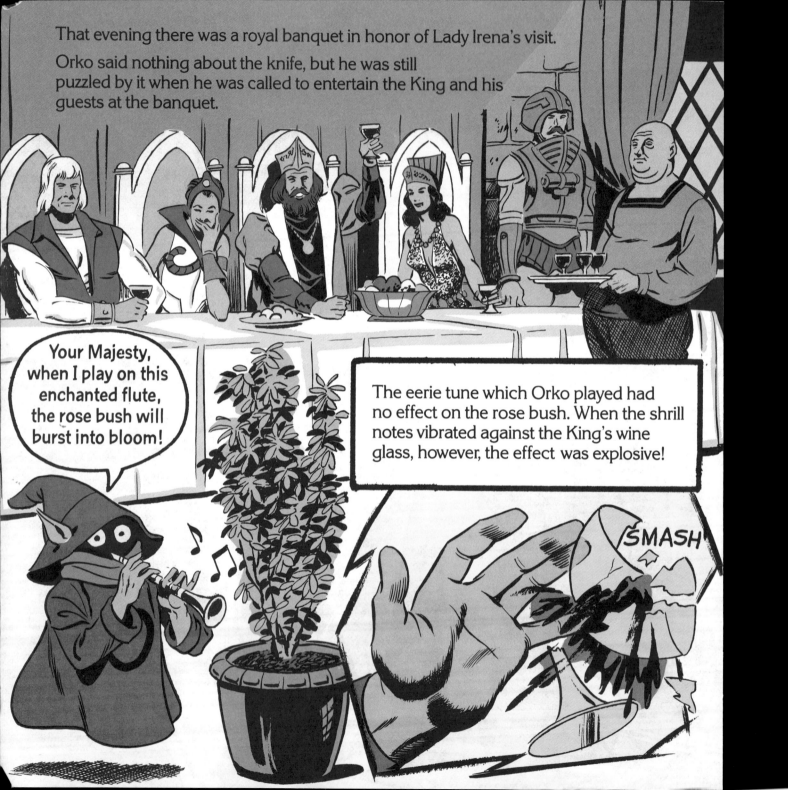

Your Majesty, when I play on this enchanted flute, the rose bush will burst into bloom!

The eerie tune which Orko played had no effect on the rose bush. When the shrill notes vibrated against the King's wine glass, however, the effect was explosive!

SMASH

"You little wretch!" screamed Irena. "Look what you did!" She seized her own goblet and hurled it at Orko. "Get back to the stables where you belong!" she cried.

Orko dropped his flute and fled.

"Why did Irena act that way?" Prince Adam wondered out loud. "It's not like her. She's always been so gentle."

"Gentle?" snapped Orko. "Do gentle ladies throw things at innocent little jesters? There's something else, Adam. Before dinner I saw her

sharpen a dagger!" said Orko. "Do gentle ladies need daggers?"

"Irena with a weapon?" said Prince Adam. "From the time we were children she has hated violence and weapons! This requires investigation!" With that, the Prince hurried away to his room.

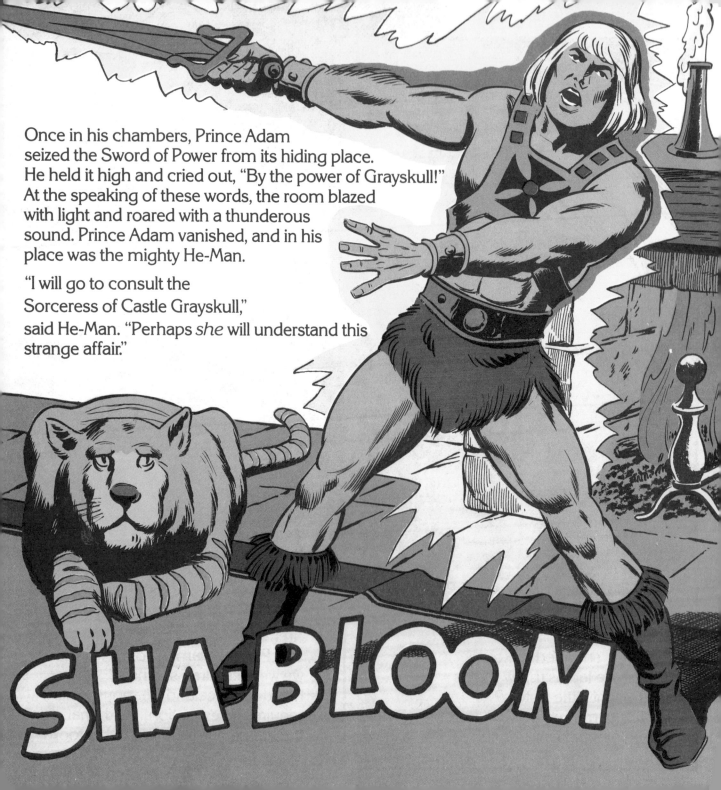

Once in his chambers, Prince Adam seized the Sword of Power from its hiding place. He held it high and cried out, "By the power of Grayskull!" At the speaking of these words, the room blazed with light and roared with a thunderous sound. Prince Adam vanished, and in his place was the mighty He-Man.

"I will go to consult the Sorceress of Castle Grayskull," said He-Man. "Perhaps *she* will understand this strange affair."

SHA·BLOOM

VLA BOOM

He-Man pointed his sword at Cringer. Magic flew from its gleaming blade. Instantly, his gentle pet tiger was transformed into the fierce Battle Cat!

He-Man and Battle Cat raced through the night to Castle Grayskull. There, the Sorceress— Guardian of Grayskull—waited. She was always ready to help He-Man in his fight against Evil.

I have been expecting you He-Man, for I sense there is trouble abroad in our land!

He-Man told the Sorceress of Irena's strange behavior.

"Perhaps Evil is masked by a fair face," said the Sorceress. "We shall see." She waved her hand and a cloud appeared.

He-Man gazed at the images in the cloud. He saw the banquet hall at the Palace. There he saw Irena entertaining the guests, playing for them on her harp.

The vision in the cloud suddenly changed, and the banquet hall was gone. In its place He-Man saw a swamp. In the swamp he saw a crystal globe where a maiden struggled in vain to get free.

"That creature at the Palace is an impostor!" cried the Sorceress. "Here is the *real* Irena!"

"A prisoner of Mer-Man!" gasped He-Man. "I've got to stop him! But first I must return to the Palace!" He thanked the Sorceress and was on his way.

He-Man's mighty Sword of Power flashed—
and the harp was destroyed forever!

NO! Not my harp!

THOOM

The Sword glowed with magical strength, numbing the creature's hand, and forcing the dagger to drop to the ground.

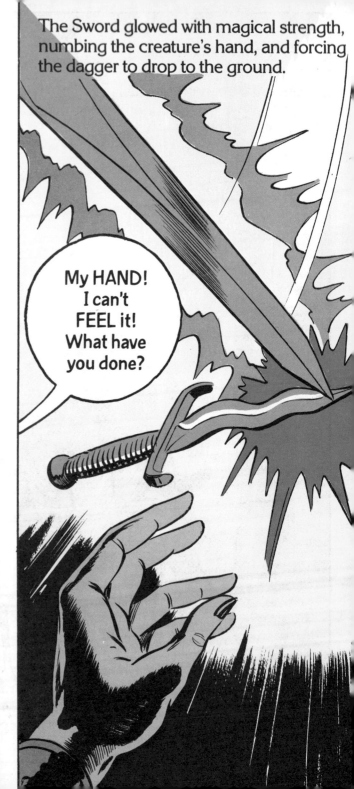

My HAND! I can't FEEL it! What have you done?

He-Man watched as the fair maiden shriveled and twisted and shrank away. Right before his eyes she became a hideous beast!

One of Skeletor's demons!

Suddenly Skeletor himself was there, and his loathsome henchmen were with him. "You come too late, He-Man," said Skeletor. "The King and his guards sleep. The kingdom is mine!"

What Skeletor did not realize was that the sleeping enchantment had ended when the harp was destroyed. The Palace instantly came alive.

Suddenly a last, desperate idea came to He-Man.

Orko's flute! The one he played at dinner! Where is it?

Here! But— the shattered goblet! of course.

Do you think there's a chance?

"Let us hope so!" replied He-Man.
"It is our *only* chance!"
He pressed the flute to
his lips and began to play.
The sound seemed to float toward
the globe, and surround it.

The next night there was another feast at the Palace, and again the Lady Irena was the guest of honor. This time it was the real Irena who sat beside the King and listened to the tune Orko piped on his marvelous flute.

This time the rose bush *did* burst into bloom!—and this time his majesty sipped his wine from a *silver* cup, so he could be *sure* it would not shatter!

"Wonderful" said Prince Adam to Teela.

She frowned. "Yes. Today's *magic* is wonderful. Yesterday's *battle* was not! Where were *you* during *that*, Adam? Why are you always off someplace whenever there's fighting to do?"

"Perhaps I prefer magic to battles," said the Prince.

Teela let out a sigh of exasperation, turned back to the entertainment and tried to enjoy herself.

Prince Adam just smiled.